T0197677

Bunny and the Rainbow

Eileen M. Foti

To order additional copies of this book, contact:
Xlibris
844-714-8691
www.Xlibris.com
Orders@Xlibris.com

ISBN: Softcover   978-1-6641-8087-1
        Hardcover   978-1-6641-8088-8
        EBook   978-1-6641-8086-4

Print information available on the last page

Rev. date: 06/18/2021

Dedication

I would like to thank my daughter, Eileen, for being my bright and beautiful rainbow

A voice called to Bunny, "Where are you going? Why are you in a hurry?"

"I'm looking for a rainbow. The sun is shining through the rain and I want to find a rainbow", said Bunny

"Who is talking to me? Where are you?" asked Bunny.

"This is Chipmunk talking to you. I am up here in the drainpipe. Why do you want to find a rainbow?

"I am tired of green grass and pink clover. I want to see all different colors. My friend, Squirrel, told me he once saw a lovely rainbow. The colors were beautiful, and I want to see one to," replied Bunny.

"Remember, not everyone has a chance to see a rainbow. Just because you run around frantically don't expect to see a rainbow arc in front of your eyes, warned Chipmunk

"If you look over in the next yard you'll see a rainbow growing in the ground, "said Snail, as the Snail family walked past Bunny

Bunny ran to the next yard. There she found a group of tulips growing along the side of the fence. The colors were bright and gorgeous. This is not a rainbow thought Bunny, and she hopped back to her own yard

"Chipmunk, are you still there?" asked Bunny

"I sure am" said Chipmunk "Did you find a rainbow?"

"NO. I found tulips of every color, but flowers are not rainbows", said Bunny.

"I think I will take a nap; all this running has made me very sleepy", yawned Bunny

"Have a nice nap", said Chipmunk quietly

Bunny closed her eyes, wiggled into the grass and fell asleep.

In her dream, Bunny saw a rainbow! She ran to the end of the rainbow and hopped on.

She walked up the arc of red

She slid down the arc of orange

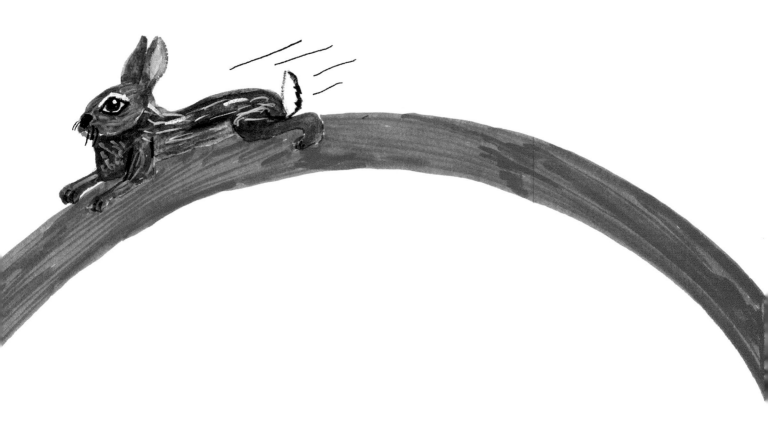

She ran along the arc of yellow

Then Bunny slipped and grabbed onto the arc of green.

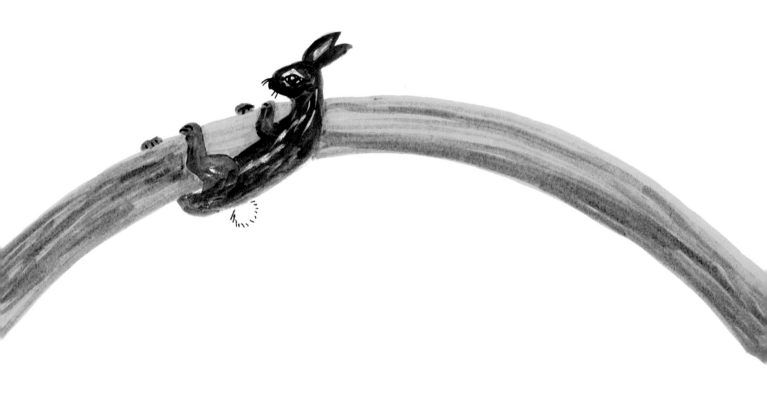

She went up the arc of blue and sat down. She was so happy to be able to sit and look over the rainbow.

Bunny then laid down on the arc of indigo, and enjoyed its' beauty.

The last arc was violet, and Bunny thought it was the most beautiful color of all. She hung over the violet arc to study it

Bunny woke up with a smile on her face.

"Hi", said Chipmunk, "I'm over here in the grass. Did you have a nice nap?"

"Yes" Bunny answered

"Are you still going to look for a rainbow?" asked Chipmunk

"No", said the Bunny, "Like you once said, "Not everyone will see a rainbow, but we can all dream about one!

Now you can make your own rainbow!

Just color the 7 arcs below, starting with red, then orange, then yellow, then green, then blue, then indigo, then violet and you will have your own rainbow!

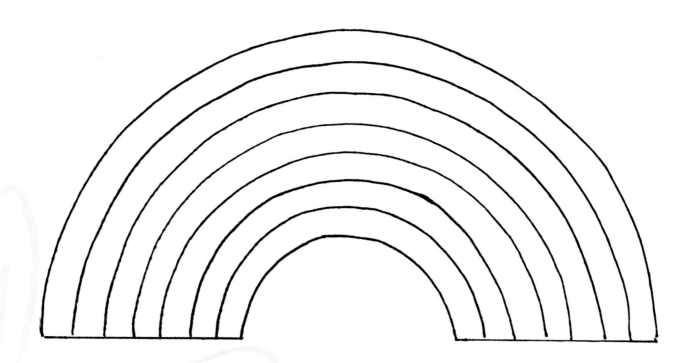

Printed in the United States
by Baker & Taylor Publisher Services